ME and UNCLE ROMIE

A Story Inspired by the Life and Art of Romare Bearden

by **CLAIRE HARTFIELD**
paintings by **JEROME LAGARRIGUE**

DIAL BOOKS FOR YOUNG READERS NEW YORK

To my daughters, Emily, Caroline, and Corinne
—C.H.

This book is dedicated to Jean and Lillian Lagarrigue, and to Ryan Glover
and his family. Thank you for your support and generosity.
—J.L.

Published by Dial Books for Young Readers
A division of Penguin Putnam Inc.
345 Hudson Street
New York, New York 10014

10 9 8 7 6 5 4 3 2 1

Library of Congress Cataloging-in-Publication Data
Hartfield, Claire.
Me and Uncle Romie: a story inspired by the life and art of Romare Bearden/
by Claire Hartfield; paintings by Jerome Lagarrigue.
p. cm.
Summary: A boy from North Carolina spends the summer in
New York City visiting the neighborhood of Harlem, where his uncle,
collage artist Romare Bearden, grew up. Includes a biographical sketch
of Bearden and instructions on making a story collage.
ISBN 0-8037-2520-5 (hc.)
1. Bearden, Romare, 1911–1988—Juvenile fiction.
[1. Bearden, Romare, 1911–1988—Fiction. 2. Artists—Fiction.
3. Uncles—Fiction. 4. Afro-Americans—Fiction.
5. Harlem (New York, N.Y.)—Fiction.]
I. Lagarrigue, Jerome, ill. II. Title.
PZ7.H2625Hap 2002
[E]—dc21 99-41390

The art was created using acrylic paint and collage elements.

*I*t was the summer Mama had the twins that I first met my uncle Romie. The doctor had told Mama she had to stay off her feet till the babies got born. Daddy thought it was a good time for me to visit Uncle Romie and his wife, Aunt Nanette, up north in New York City. But I wasn't so sure. Mama had told me that Uncle Romie was some kind of artist, and he didn't have any kids. I'd seen his picture too. He looked scary—a bald-headed, fierce-eyed giant. No, I wasn't sure about this visit at all.

The day before I left home was a regular North Carolina summer day. "A good train-watching day," my friend B.J. said.

We waited quietly in the grass beside the tracks. B.J. heard it first. "It's a'coming," he said. Then I heard it too—a low rumbling, building to a roar. *WHOOO—OOO!*

"The *Piedmont*!" we shouted as the train blasted past.

"I'm the greatest train-watcher ever," B.J. boasted.

"Yeah," I answered, "but tomorrow I'll be *riding* a train. I'm the lucky one."

Lucky, I thought as we headed home. *Maybe.*

That evening I packed my suitcase. Voices drifted up from the porch below.

"Romie's got that big art show coming up," Mama said quietly. "I hope he's not too busy for James, especially on his birthday."

"Romie's a good man," Daddy replied. "And Nanette'll be there too."

The light faded. Mama called me into her bedroom. "Where's my good-night kiss?" she said.

I curled up next to her. "I'll miss the way you make my birthday special, Mama. Your lemon cake and the baseball game."

"Well," Mama sighed, "it won't be those things. But Uncle Romie and Aunt Nanette are family, and they love you too. It'll still be a good birthday, honey."

Mama pulled me close. Her voice sang soft and low. Later, in my own bed, I listened as crickets began their song and continued into the night.

The next morning I hugged Mama good-bye, and Daddy and I headed for the train. He got me seated, then stood waving at me from the outside. I held tight to the jar of pepper jelly Mama had given me for Uncle Romie.

"ALL A-BOARD!" The conductor's voice crackled over the loud-speaker.

The train pulled away. *Chug-a-chug-a-chug-a-chug.* I watched my town move past my window—bright-colored houses, chickens strutting across the yards, flowers everywhere.

After a while I felt hungry. Daddy had packed me a lunch and a dinner to eat one at a time. I ate almost everything at once. Then my belly felt tight and I was kind of sleepy. I closed my eyes and dreamed about Mama and Daddy getting ready for those babies. Would they even miss me?

Later, when I woke up, I ate the last bit of my dinner and thought about my birthday. Would they make my lemon cake and take me to a baseball game in New York?

The sky turned from dark blue to black. I was getting sleepy all over again.

"We're almost there, son," the man next to me said.

Then I saw it . . . New York City. Buildings stretching up to the sky. So close together. Not like North Carolina at all.

"Penn Station! Watch your step," the conductor said, helping me down to the platform. I did like Daddy said and found a spot for myself close to the train. Swarms of people rushed by. Soon I heard a silvery voice call my name. This had to be Aunt Nanette. I turned and saw her big smile reaching out to welcome me.

She took my hand and guided me through the rushing crowds onto an underground train called the subway. "This will take us right home," she explained.

Home was like nothing I'd ever seen before. No regular houses anywhere. Just big buildings and stores of all kinds—in the windows I saw paints, fabrics, radios, and TVs.

We turned into the corner building and climbed the stairs to the apartment—five whole flights up. *Whew!* I tried to catch my breath while Aunt Nanette flicked on the lights.

"Uncle Romie's out talking to some people about his big art show that's coming up. He'll be home soon," Aunt Nanette said. She set some milk and a plate of cookies for me on the table. "Your uncle's working very hard, so we won't see much of him for a while. His workroom—we call it his studio—is in the front of our apartment. That's where he keeps all the things he needs to make his art."

"Doesn't he just paint?" I asked.

"Uncle Romie is a collage artist," Aunt Nanette explained. "He uses paints, yes. But also photographs, newspapers, cloth. He cuts and pastes them onto a board to make his paintings."

"That sounds kinda easy," I said.

Aunt Nanette laughed.

"Well, there's a little more to it than that, James. When you see the paintings, you'll understand. Come, let's get you to bed."

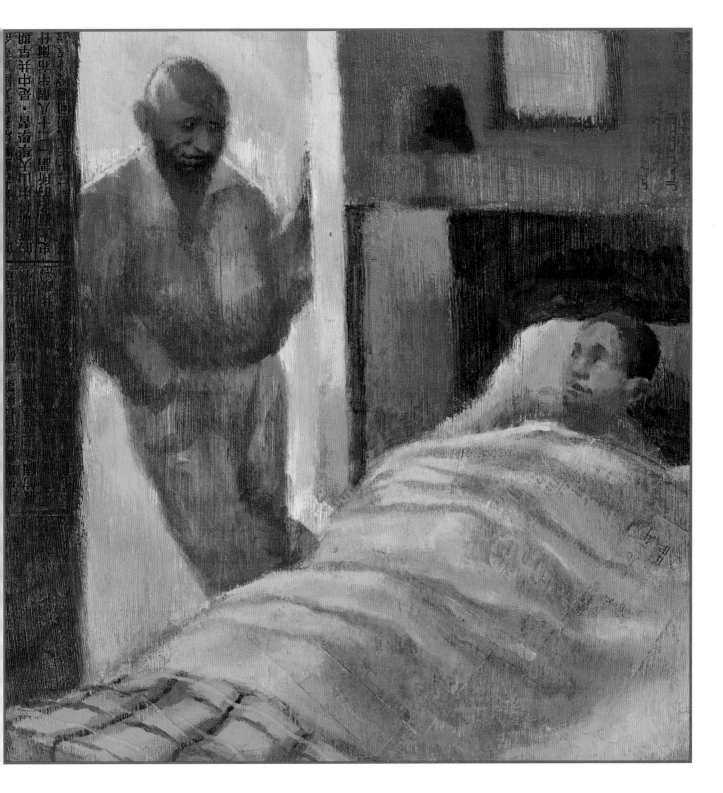

Lying in the dark, I heard heavy footsteps in the hall. A giant stared at me from the doorway. "Hello there, James." Uncle Romie's voice was deep and loud, like thunder. "Thanks for the pepper jelly," he boomed. "You have a good sleep, now." Then he disappeared down the hall.

The next morning the door to Uncle Romie's studio was closed. But Aunt Nanette had plans for both of us. "Today we're going to a neighborhood called Harlem," she said. "It's where Uncle Romie lived as a boy."

Harlem was full of people walking, working, shopping, eating. Some were watching the goings-on from fire escapes. Others were sitting out on stoops greeting folks who passed by—just like the people back home calling out hellos from their front porches. Most everybody seemed to know Aunt Nanette. A lot of them asked after Uncle Romie too.

We bought peaches at the market, then stopped to visit awhile. I watched some kids playing stickball. "Go on, get in that game," Aunt Nanette said, gently pushing me over to join them. When I was all hot and sweaty, we cooled off with double chocolate scoops from the ice cream man. Later we shared some barbecue on a rooftop way up high. I felt like I was on top of the world.

As the days went by, Aunt Nanette took me all over the city—we rode a ferry boat to the Statue of Liberty . . . zoomed 102 floors up at the Empire State Building . . . window-shopped the fancy stores on Fifth Avenue . . . gobbled hot dogs in Central Park.

But it was Harlem that I liked best. I played stickball with the kids again . . . and on a really hot day a whole bunch of us ran through the icy cold water that sprayed out hard from the fire hydrant. In the evenings Aunt Nanette and I sat outside listening to the street musicians playing their saxophone songs.

On rainy days I wrote postcards and helped out around the apartment. I told Aunt Nanette about the things I liked to do back home—about baseball games, train-watching, my birthday. She told me about the special Caribbean lemon and mango cake she was going to make.

My uncle Romie stayed hidden away in his studio. But I wasn't worried anymore. Aunt Nanette would make my birthday special.

4 . . . 3 . . . 2 . . . 1 . . . My birthday was almost here!

And then Aunt Nanette got a phone call.

"An old aunt has died, James. I have to go away for her funeral. But don't you worry. Uncle Romie will spend your birthday with you. It'll be just fine."

That night Aunt Nanette kissed me good-bye. I knew it would not be fine at all. Uncle Romie didn't know about cakes or baseball games or anything except his dumb old paintings. My birthday was ruined.

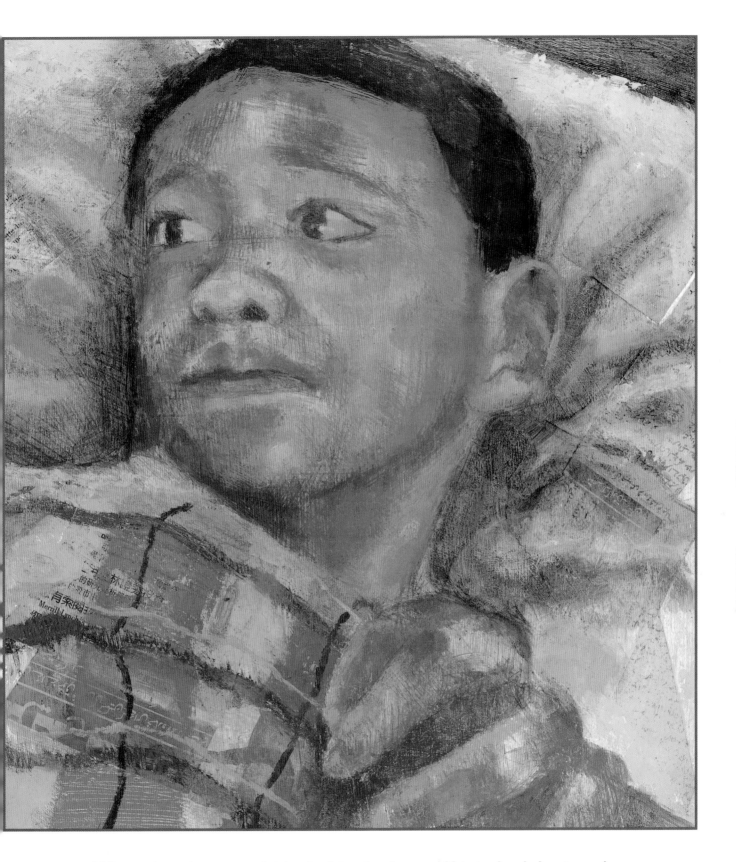

When the sky turned black, I tucked myself into bed. I missed Mama and Daddy so much. I listened to the birds on the rooftop— their songs continued into the night.

The next morning everything was quiet. I crept out of bed and into the hall. For the first time the door to Uncle Romie's studio stood wide open. What a glorious mess! There were paints and scraps all over the floor, and around the edges were huge paintings with all sorts of pieces pasted together.

I saw saxophones, birds, fire escapes, and brown faces. *It's Harlem,* I thought. *The people, the music, the rooftops, and the stoops.* Looking at Uncle Romie's paintings, I could *feel* Harlem—its beat and bounce.

Then there was one that was different. Smaller houses, flowers, and trains. "That's home!" I shouted.

"Yep," Uncle Romie said, smiling, from the doorway. "That's the Carolina I remember."

"Mama says you visited your grandparents there most every summer when you were a kid," I said.

"I sure did, James. *Mmm.* Now that's the place for pepper jelly. Smeared thick on biscuits. And when Grandma wasn't looking . . . I'd sneak some on a spoon."

"Daddy and I do that too!" I told him.

We laughed together, then walked to the kitchen for a breakfast feast—eggs, bacon, grits, and biscuits.

"James, you've got me remembering the pepper jelly lady. People used to line up down the block to buy her preserves."

"Could you put someone like that in one of your paintings?" I asked.

"I guess I could." Uncle Romie nodded. "Yes, that's a memory just right for sharing. What a good idea, James. Now let's get this birthday going!"

He brought out two presents from home. I tore into the packages while he got down the pepper jelly and two huge spoons. Mama and Daddy had picked out just what I wanted—a special case for my baseball cards, and a model train for me to build.

"Pretty cool," said Uncle Romie. "I used to watch the trains down in North Carolina, you know."

How funny to picture big Uncle Romie lying on his belly!

"B.J. and me, we have contests to see who can hear the trains first."

"Hey, I did that too. You know, it's a funny thing, James. People live in all sorts of different places and families. But the things we care about are pretty much the same. Like favorite foods, special songs, games, stories . . . and like birthdays." Uncle Romie held up two tickets to a baseball game!

It turns out Uncle Romie knows all about baseball—he was even a star pitcher in college. We got our mitts and set off for the game.

Way up in the bleachers, we shared a bag of peanuts, cracking the shells with our teeth and keeping our mitts ready in case a home run ball came our way. That didn't happen—but we sure had fun.

Aunt Nanette came home that night. She lit the candles and we all shared my Caribbean birthday cake.

After that, Uncle Romie had to work a lot again. But at the end of each day he let me sit with him in his studio and talk. Daddy was right. Uncle Romie is a good man.

The day of the big art show finally came. I watched the people laughing and talking, walking slowly around the room from painting to painting. I walked around myself, listening to their conversations.

"Remember our first train ride from Chicago to New York?" one lady asked her husband.

"That guitar-playing man reminds me of my uncle Joe," said another.

All these strangers talking to each other about their families and friends and special times, and all because of how my uncle Romie's paintings reminded them of these things.

Later that night Daddy called. I had a brand-new brother and sister. Daddy said they were both bald and made a lot of noise. But he sounded happy and said how they all missed me.

This time Aunt Nanette and Uncle Romie took me to the train station.

"Here's a late birthday present for you, James," Uncle Romie said, holding out a package. "Open it on the train, why don't you. It'll help pass the time on the long ride home."

I waved out the window to Uncle Romie and Aunt Nanette until I couldn't see them anymore. Then I ripped off the wrappings!

And there was my summer in New York. Bright sky in one corner, city lights at night in another. Tall buildings. Baseball ticket stubs. The label from the pepper jelly jar. And trains. One going toward the skyscrapers. Another going away.

Back home, I lay in the soft North Carolina grass. It was the first of September, almost Uncle Romie's birthday. I watched the birds streak across the sky.

Rooftop birds, I thought. *Back home from their summer in New York, just like me.* Watching them, I could still feel the city's beat inside my head.

A feather drifted down from the sky. In the garden tiger lilies bent in the wind. *Uncle Romie's favorite flowers.* I yanked off a few blossoms. And then I was off on a treasure hunt, collecting things that reminded me of Uncle Romie.

I painted and pasted them together on a big piece of cardboard. Right in the middle I put the train schedule. And at the top I wrote:

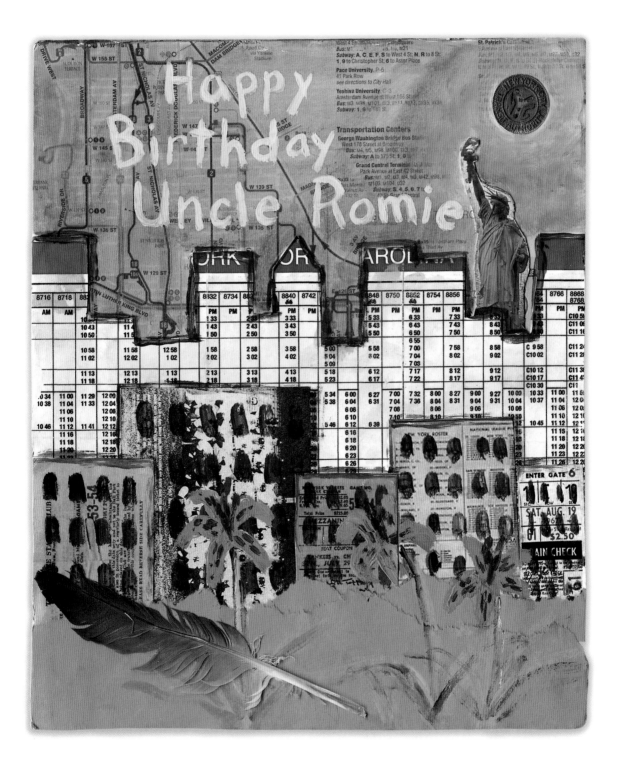

MAKING COLLAGE

Like James in *Me and Uncle Romie,* you can make wonderful storytelling collages by applying methods similar to those Romare Bearden used to create his work.

Choosing a Story or Theme

To begin your project, pick a story or theme for your collage. Do you want to tell about something that happened to you, someone you know, or someone you've heard about? Or would you rather make up a story, maybe about something you'd like to see happen? Is there a theme that would make a fun collage—things that make you laugh, things you do at bedtime, a list of wishes, favorite songs? To get ideas, try to think of people, places, and memories that mean a lot to you.

Once you've settled on the story or theme, think about images you can use in your collage to illustrate what you want to say. What do you want in the picture? People? Animals? What are they doing? Where are they? What do they see, hear, smell, taste and feel? It might help to make a list—but remember, it's okay to add things or change your mind.

Materials You Will Need

- A board or thick piece of paper (such as cardboard or sturdy construction paper) to use as the collage background. It can be any shape you want, but make sure it is the size that you want your final collage to be.
- Paints, colored markers, or crayons.
- Glue or paste.
- Anything that can be glued or pasted onto your paper or board can also be used to create your collage story. Some materials to consider include photos, pictures from magazines, cloth, beads, different kinds of paper (a label, part of a cereal box, wrapping paper), buttons, wood, or documents (a newspaper, invitation, program, ticket stub). Of course, you may add any other objects that seem right for your work (a lock of hair? a drinking straw? stickers? a ribbon?).
- A small amount of non-toxic spray or lacquer, to protect your collage when it is finished.

Creating Your Collage

Start by deciding whether or not it's important to have the images you'll be using in any particular order. If it is, you can lay them out to get an idea of how they will look together.

Next, paint or color the background on your paper or board. Use colors you want to peek through in the finished picture.

Then begin to create your story or theme by cutting and pasting your objects onto the background. You may want to use different materials to create a single image. For example, you can group together buttons, string, and magazine cutouts to make the eyes, nose, and mouth of a face.

When you are finished, you can spray or brush the lacquer over the entire collage to protect it and give it a nice shiny look.

Ideas for Special Ways to Present Your Collage

You can share your finished collage with your family, friends, and class-mates. Here are some ways to do this:

- Using collage can make school projects more fun. You could use your collage to tell about something you are studying. Or you might create a collage to share a personal story with your class.
- Collages make great gifts! You can make a collage like James, or . . .
- Create a collage on the top of a box that can be used as a jewelry box, treasure chest, or keepsake box.
- Create a decorative pencil cup or vase by making a collage that can be wrapped around and glued onto a clean, empty food can or jar.
- Create handmade collage wrapping paper.
- Create your own greeting cards—for birthdays, holidays, to thank, cheer up, or just let people know you are thinking of them, or for any special occasion (You Made the Team!, I'll Miss You, Congratulations on Your Great Report Card).

These are just some of the possibilities of what you can say with collage art. Best of all, whatever you create will be special because you are sharing a part of who you are.

HAVE FUN

AUTHOR'S NOTE

This story, which is fictional, was inspired by the storytelling quality of Romare Bearden's art and has incorporated many of the basic facts of his life.

Romare Bearden was born in Charlotte, North Carolina, on September 2, 1911. He spent his early childhood in Charlotte and even after he moved north spent many summers there. When he was still a child, his family moved to Harlem in New York City. This was during the 1920s, a period called the Harlem Renaissance, when many famous African American writers, musicians, and artists lived and worked in Harlem. Bearden often sat out on the stoop of his apartment building, listening to music, getting to know his neighbors, and taking in the scene. In 1954, Bearden married Nanette Rohan, whose family is from the Caribbean island of St. Martin.

As Bearden grew to be a young man, he chose painting to express the African American experience as he knew it. He experimented with many different ways of painting, finally deciding that collage was the best form for expressing his ideas. Many of his paintings are on exhibit in museums and galleries across the United States. His work has also appeared in several children's books. In 1987 Romare Bearden was awarded the National Medal of Arts by President Ronald Reagan.

Bearden died on March 12, 1988.

The Pepper Jelly Lady

The Romare Bearden Foundation supports this book as a way to introduce his art and personal history to children. You can learn more by contacting them at:

The Romare Bearden Foundation
305 Seventh Avenue • New York, NY 10001 • (212) 924-0455
www.beardenfoundation.org

panel from *The Block*